Venus
The Forbidden Love of Taurean's and Librans

By India Cunningham

Words 20,739

Introduction: The Bridge Between Worlds

On Earth, she was Iris an ordinary young woman, recovering from a life altering accident. Her days were filled with the familiar rhythms of family, friends, and the quiet hum of normalcy. But deep within her heart, she carried the weight of another identity, another life.

On Venus, she was Ife the daughter of royalty, a keeper of secrets, and the bearer of forbidden love. Her memories of this celestial world were fragmented but powerful, whispering tales of joy and heartbreak, of unity and division.

As Iris navigated her Earthly existence, the boundaries between her two worlds began to blur. Love, loss, and destiny wove a tapestry that connected both lives, revealing a purpose far greater than she ever imagined.

Caught between two realms, Iris must embrace her dual identity to become the bridge between Earth and Venus a bridge forged by love, tested by loyalty, and strengthened by the courage to face the unknown.

Chapter One: The Beginning

Hello, Iris. Can you hear me?

Doctor Grant's voice was calm but firm as he examined her unresponsive form. I believe she's slipping into a coma. Iris... Iris, stay with me!

Two Months Later...

Iris, honey, can you hear me?

A faint groan escaped her lips as her eyes fluttered open. Confusion clouded her face as she looked around the room.

Whose Iris? she murmured.

Mrs. Love gasped. Honey, you are Iris! Turning toward the hallway, she yelled, Doctor Grant, come quick! Something's wrong!

The doctor hurried in. What's going on?

She doesn't remember who she is! Mrs. Love cried.

Doctor Grant's expression softened. Mrs. Love, please stay calm. I know this is upsetting, but it's not uncommon. Patients who've experienced severe head trauma and comas can wake up with amnesia. The good news is that most recover their memories over time.

Mrs. Love's voice trembled. How can I calm down when my daughter doesn't even recognize me?

I understand, Doctor Grant said. But there are steps we can take. I'll refer you to a therapist who specializes in memory recovery. They'll guide Iris through the process.

Thank you, Doctor, Mrs. Love replied, wiping her tears.

Later that day, Mrs. Love sat beside her daughter's hospital bed. Iris, we'll meet with the therapist soon. Afterward, we'll go to your place to get some clothes, and you'll stay with me until you recover.

I've told you, Iris snapped, her voice firm, my name isn't Iris it's Ife. And I don't need a therapist. My memories are perfectly fine, thank you very much.

Mrs. Love sighed. Well, Ife or whoever you think you are we're going to the therapist. Doctor's orders.

Whatever.

The Therapist

Hello, Ms. Smith, Mrs. Love said as they entered the office. This is my daughter, Iris.

Ife corrected her sharply. My name is *Ife*, not Iris. And this woman is not my mother.

Ms. Smith smiled gently. No worries, Ms. Love. I've got it from here.

Turning to Ife, she extended a hand. It's very nice to meet you, Ife. I understand you've been through a lot, a car accident, a coma… I can't imagine how overwhelming that must be. Would you like to talk about it?

Ife shrugged. What's there to talk about? I don't remember the accident. The doctors said it was brutal, though.

And your mother is worried because you insist, she isn't your real mom.

She isn't, Ife said firmly. Everyone wants me to 'recover my memories, but the truth is, my memories *are* back.

Ms. Smith tilted her head curiously. What do you mean by that?

Ife glanced away, her exhaustion evident. I'm tired. Can we continue this another day?

Of course, Ms. Smith said warmly. We'll meet again soon.

Iris, you didn't have to be rude to Mrs. Smith, Mrs. Love said as they left the office. She was only trying to help.

I wasn't being rude, Ife replied wearily. I've had a long day, and I'm tired. And like I told her, if you can't address me by my name, I won't speak to you. You're hurting my feelings, Ife, Mrs. Love said, her voice breaking. I *am* your mother, I have proof.

Ife paused, her eyes narrowing. Okay, you have my attention. Where's your proof?

After we pick up some clothes from your apartment, I'll show you your baby pictures back at my house.

Ife hesitated, then nodded. Fine. Ife, I have a question.

What is it?

If I'm not your mother, then who is?

A flicker of determination crossed her face. My mother's name is Empress Ayao, the Goddess of Air, from the Libran Royal Family.

Wow, this is my place? Ife asked as they entered the apartment. It's nice. Do I have to go back with you?

Yes, you do, Mrs. Love replied firmly.

Ruff! Ruff!

Startled, Ife jumped back. What is *that*? That's your dog, Royal! Mrs. Love laughed. My dog? There's nothing royal about a dog. Now, if it were a kitten, that'd make more sense. As Mrs. Love packed, Ife muttered, can we leave the dog here? No, Ife. Royal comes with us. Fine. But don't expect me to like it. Later that evening, Ife lay in bed, staring at the ceiling. The distant sound of laughter floated from the living room where her newfound family watched TV together. Her mind swirled with conflicting emotions frustration at the gaps in her memory and an inexplicable warmth at the care these strangers showed her.

A soft knock at the door broke her thoughts.

Come in, she called.

Imani peeked in, holding a tray with a mug of tea. Hey, I brought you something to help you sleep. Mom always makes this when one of us can't relax.

Ife sat up slowly, a small smile tugging at her lips. Thanks, Imani.

Imani set the tray down and perched on the edge of the bed. You know, it must be hard waking up and not knowing anyone. I can't even imagine what that feels like.

It's... strange, Ife admitted. I keep trying to force myself to remember, but the harder I try, the more my head hurts. And yet, there's this... other part of me. A place where I know exactly who I am.

Imani tilted her head curiously. You mean Venus?

Yes, Ife said, her voice soft but certain. On Venus, everything makes sense. I'm Ife, daughter of Empress Ayao. I'm the eldest sibling of the Libran royal family. But here... here, I feel like a puzzle piece in the wrong box. Imani reached out and squeezed her hand. Well, for what it's worth, we're happy you're here even if you think you're from another world. Maybe the memories you have of Venus are connected to your life here somehow. Like dreams or stories, you told yourself.

Maybe, Ife replied, though her heart whispered otherwise. The next morning, the family gathered in the living room to watch home videos. Ife sat on the couch, sandwiched between Imani and Jake, with Royal sprawled lazily at her feet.

Alright, pumpkin, Mr. Love said, clicking play. Let's see if these sparks anything.

The screen flickered to life, showing a toddler Ife then Iris chasing a giggling Imani through a sunlit park. A younger Mr. and Mrs. Love sat on a bench, cheering them on.

That's you! Imani exclaimed, pointing at the screen. You were always so fast. I couldn't ever catch you.

Ife watched in silence, her brow furrowing. There was something so familiar about the laughter, the warmth, the carefree joy in the scene.

As the footage continued, Ife leaned forward, captivated. I look... so happy, she whispered.

You were, Mrs. Love said, her voice thick with emotion. You lit up every room you entered, Iris. You still do.

Ife's throat tightened, and she turned away from the screen. It's overwhelming, she admitted, blinking back tears. I don't remember any of this, but I feel it like a faint echo of something I've lost. Take your time, Mr. Love said gently. We're here for you, no matter how long it takes. Later that night, Ife couldn't sleep. She sat by the window, gazing at the moonlit sky. The stars seemed to shimmer brighter than usual, as if whispering secrets only she could hear.

Imani tiptoed in, her presence quiet but comforting. Can't sleep again?

Ife shook her head. It's strange. Watching those videos earlier... I felt like I was on the edge of remembering something important. But then it slipped away, like sand through my fingers.

Imani joined her by the window, resting her chin on her knees. Maybe it's not about forcing yourself to remember. Maybe you just need to let it come naturally.

Ife glanced at her. Do you really believe that?

I do, Imani said with a smile. And I believe in you.

For the first time, Ife felt a flicker of hope. Thank you, Imani. I don't say it enough, but I'm grateful for you and everyone else. Even... Ms. Love.

Imani laughed. You mean Mom.

Yeah, Ife said softly. Mom.

Chapter Two: Memories and Questions

As the weeks went by, Ife tried to recover her memories as Iris. One day as the sunlight filtered through the curtains as the family prepared for another busy day. Mrs. Love stood at the stove flipping pancakes, the sweet aroma filling the kitchen. Imani sat at the table scrolling through her phone, while Jake lay half asleep on the couch, his arm draped over his eyes.

Ife walked in, rubbing the sleep from her eyes. She looked groggy but alert. Morning, she mumbled.

Everyone turned to her, their expressions a mix of relief and curiosity.

Good morning, pumpkin! Mr. Love greeted cheerfully. How are you feeling today?

Better, Ife admitted, sliding into a chair beside Imani. A little weird, though.

Mrs. Love placed a plate of pancakes in front of her. Weird how?

Ife hesitated, glancing around the room before speaking. I feel like I'm two different people, she said slowly. There's Iris the girl in all the home videos, the one you all know. And then there's Ife, daughter of Empress Ayao, living on Venus. I have memories of both, but they don't always make sense together.

The room fell silent.

Jake sat up, eyes wide. Wait so you remember being Iris and you remember being Ife? Like... two whole lives?

Mr. Love exchanged a look with Mrs. Love, his face creased with concern.

Mrs. Love turned back to Ife, her voice gentle but serious. What exactly do you remember, honey?

Ife took a deep breath. This morning, A memory came back to me, not from Venus, but from here. From when I was Iris.

Everyone leaned in slightly, waiting.

I was in the backyard, Ife began, her gaze distant. I must've been six or seven. It was summer, and Dad was helping me ride my bike without training wheels. I remember feeling terrified of falling, but then he let go, and for a few seconds, I was doing it. I was riding all on my own. A small smile played at her lips. I felt so free like I was flying. But then I looked back and realized he wasn't holding on anymore, and I panicked. I fell and scraped my knee.

Mr. Love let out a soft chuckle. I remember that day. You were so mad at me for letting go.

I was, Ife admitted. But when you picked me up, you told me I did it that I had ridden all by myself, even if it was just for a moment. And that made me want to try again. She exhaled slowly. I don't know why, but it felt important... like it was reminding me of something.

Imani was the first to break the silence. So, you're saying you remember being Iris, living your life here... but you also remember being Ife on Venus?

Yes. Ife nodded, gripping her fork. Both memories feel real. It's like I'm both at the same time.

Jake ran a hand through his hair. That's... crazy.

Mr. Love let out a slow breath. I don't even know how to process that.

Mrs. Love placed a hand on Ife's shoulder, her expression full of warmth and understanding. No matter what you remember or who you feel like right now, you're still our daughter. And we love you.

Ife felt something loosen in her chest. That's all I needed to hear.

After breakfast, the family piled into the car, heading to the pet shop to pick up Royal. But even as they laughed and talked on the way, Ife couldn't shake the feeling that the memory meant more than just a childhood moment it was a bridge between the person she had been and the one she was becoming.

ROYAL! Ife exclaimed as soon as they stepped into the pet shop. The golden furred dog perked up at the sound of her voice, his tail wagging furiously as he trotted toward her.

She dropped to her knees, wrapping her arms around him as he licked her face enthusiastically. Okay, okay, I missed you too! she laughed, trying to dodge his eager kisses.

Ms. Evelyn, the groomer, chuckled as she approached. He was such a good boy during his grooming. I can tell he loves being pampered.

He does, Ife said, running a hand through Royal's freshly brushed fur. "Thanks for taking care of him, Ms. Evelyn.

Anytime, dear, Ms. Evelyn replied with a warm smile. He's one of my favorite clients.

Royal barked happily, trotting beside Ife as they left the shop.

Later That Day Ife sat across from Ms. Smith in the familiar, cozy therapy room. Imani was beside her, notebook in hand, ready to take notes. Ms. Smith leaned forward slightly, her expression kind but curious. So, Ife, your mom told me some incredible news. She said your memories are back. How are you feeling about that?

Ife exhaled, choosing her words carefully. I feel... complicated. I remember everything now both my life here and my life on Venus. It's overwhelming.

Ms. Smith nodded. That's understandable. Having two sets of memories must feel like carrying two lives at once.

It does, Ife agreed. But they're not separate. Somehow, they're connected. My memories of Venus feel real, not like dreams or fantasies. And yet, here I am, living this life as Iris.

Ms. Smith studied her for a moment. Tell me more about Venus.

Ife took a deep breath. On Venus, I was royalty the eldest daughter of Empress Ayao, the Goddess of Air. Our world was beautiful, balanced, and harmonious. Everyone there belonged to either the Taurean or Libran families, and our society thrived on that duality.

Imani's eyes widened. That sounds amazing.

Ife glanced at her sister, a thoughtful look in her eyes. It was. But I don't think I was sent here just to remember. There's something more... like a purpose I haven't figured out yet.

Ms. Smith tapped her pen against her notepad. That's an important realization. Instead of just focusing on who you were, maybe it's time to ask yourself: Who are you meant to become?

The question lingered in the air, settling deep in Ife's mind.

It was, Ife said wistfully. But it wasn't perfect. There was always tension between the two families, and as the eldest child, I was expected to unite them. I think that's why I feel so torn now. Part of me feels like I failed there, and that failure followed me here.

Ms. Smith tilted her head. Do you believe the accident that caused your amnesia was connected to Venus in some way?

Ife hesitated. I don't know. But I can't shake the feeling that I'm here for a reason that Venus and Earth are linked somehow, and I'm the connection.

After the session, Ife and Imani met the rest of the family at a nearby park. Royal bounded ahead, chasing a frisbee Jake had thrown.

So, Jake asked, handing Ife a bottle of water, what did Ms. Smith say?

She thinks it's important for me to explore both sets of memories, Ife said, taking a sip. To figure out how they're connected.

And do you think they're connected? Mrs. Love asked, her tone curious.

I do, Ife said firmly. But I need time to figure it out. In the meantime, I want to embrace this life, with all of you. I owe it to myself and to Iris to fully live here before I can understand how Venus fits in.

Mr. Love patted her shoulder. We'll support you every step of the way, pumpkin. Ife smiled, feeling a sense of belonging she hadn't felt since waking up in the hospital. For the first time, she felt ready to bridge the gap between her two worlds. That evening, Ife sat outside on the porch, gazing at the stars. The crisp night air carried a faint breeze, and Royal lay contentedly at her feet. Imani joined her, bringing two mugs of hot cocoa.

Mind if I sit? Imani asked.

Of course not, Ife said, her gaze never leaving the sky.

They sat in silence for a moment before Ife spoke. The stars... they remind me of home.

Venus? Imani asked, her voice soft.

Ife nodded. Yes. The skies there were always alive vivid pinks and golds, with stars that shimmered like they were dancing. My father, Emperor Montu, used to say the stars were the guardians of our world, watching over us and keeping the balance.

Imani sipped her cocoa, captivated. Tell me more about him.
Emperor Montu was powerful but kind, Ife said, her voice full of reverence. He ruled with wisdom and strength, always ensuring harmony between the Taureans and Librans. But he had a mischievous side, too. He used to tell my siblings and me stories about his adventures when he was young, exploring the hidden valleys of Venus and taming wild air dragons.

Air dragons? Imani's eyes widened.

Yes, Ife said, smiling. They were massive, with translucent wings that shimmered like rainbows. My brother, Baka, always dreamed of riding one, but he was terrified of heights. Imani laughed. Sounds like Jake. So, Baka is your brother?

Yes, Ife replied. Baka was stubborn but fiercely loyal. He believed in protecting the family at all costs, even if it meant challenging our mother's decisions.

And your sister?

Lemanja, Ife said fondly. She was the dreamer. Always painting, writing poetry, or wandering through the crystal gardens. She saw beauty in everything, even in the storms that sometimes tore through our skies.

Imani leaned closer. And your best friend? You must have had one.

Princess Lewa, Ife said, her smile growing wider. She was the daughter of Empress Oduwa, the Taurean ruler. Lewa and I were inseparable. We were supposed to be rivals, given the tensions between our families, but we couldn't care less. We'd sneak out of the palace together to explore the golden forests and play in the sky ponds. She had this contagious laugh that could brighten even the darkest day.

Imani's expression softened. You must miss them.

I do, Ife admitted. But remembering them... it feels like they're still with me somehow.

Dreams and Echoes

That night, Ife dreamed of Venus. She was standing in the royal courtyard, surrounded by towering crystal spires that shimmered in the sunlight. Her father,

Emperor Montu, stood at the edge of the courtyard, his arms outstretched as a young Baka clung to his back, laughing nervously.

Hold tight, son! Montu called, leaping into the air. An enormous air dragon swooped down, catching them on its back.

Ife laughed as she watched her brother's terror turn to exhilaration. Beside her, Lemanja sketched the scene, her hands moving deftly over a glowing parchment.

Ife! a familiar voice called.

She turned to see Princess Lewa running toward her, her silver hair glinting in the sunlight. Come on! There's a new sky pond near the cliffs we must see it before it disappears!
Let's go! Ife shouted, grabbing her hand and running with her.

The dream shifted, and Ife found herself standing in a vast hall filled with golden light. Her mother, Empress Ayao, stood at the center, her regal presence commanding the room.

Ife, Empress Ayao called, her voice echoing, you are the bridge. You must bring harmony, not only to Venus but to the worlds beyond.

Ife awoke with a start, her heart pounding. She sat up, her breath quick and shallow, as fragments of the dream lingered in her mind.

What did she mean? Ife whispered to herself.

A soft knock at the door pulled her from her thoughts. Come in, she called.

Imani peeked in. I heard you moving around. Are you okay?

I'm fine, Ife said, though her voice trembled slightly. I just had... a dream. A memory, really.

Imani sat on the edge of the bed. Tell me about it.

Ife recounted the dream, her words flowing like a river. By the time she finished, Imani was staring at her, wide eyed.
That's incredible, Imani said. Your mom Empress Ayao said you're a bridge. What do you think she meant?
I'm not sure, Ife admitted. But I think it has something to do with why I'm here. Maybe the accident wasn't just an accident. Maybe I was meant to come to Earth to bring balance between the two worlds.

Imani reached out and took her hand. If anyone can figure it out, it's you. And I'll be right here to help.

Chapter Three: The Feast of Connection

It had been a few days since Ife's dream of Venus, and her memories were beginning to surface more vividly. Sitting in the living room with her family, she found herself recounting one such memory.

You know, Ife began, her voice tinged with nostalgia, on Venus, the Taureans were famous for their feasts. They weren't just meals they were celebrations of life, harmony, and community.

Mrs. Love looked up from her knitting, intrigued. What were they like?

Ife smiled faintly. They were grand. Tables stretched as far as the eye could see, laden with fruits, pastries, and delicacies you can't even imagine. The Taureans believed in abundance and joy, and their feasts reflected that. My best friend, Princess Lewa, always snuck me the first slice of starfruit pie before anyone else could get to it.

Jake grinned. Sounds like the kind of party I'd love to crash.

They weren't just about food, Ife continued, her tone more serious. The feasts were a way to bring the two royal families together. For a time, there was true unity between the Taureans and Librans. My father worked hard to maintain that harmony.

Imani leaned closer. What happened to change it? Ife hesitated, her gaze dropping. Ambition. Greed. Corruption. Some families wanted more power, and they didn't care who they hurt to get it.

As Ife spoke, another memory surfaced one that made her shiver. She took a deep breath, steadying herself.

There was a time, she said softly, when my father had to bring justice to a family that had strayed from the path of honor. A young girl came to the palace, trembling, her face pale as moonlight. She told us her father's friend had... touched her. Kissed her. She tried to tell her parents, but they didn't believe her. The man had already lied, saying she had kissed him instead.

The room fell silent, the weight of her words settling over them.

My father didn't hesitate, Ife said, her voice steady but low. He summoned the man and the girl's parents to the throne room. He listened to both sides, but he knew the truth in his heart. The girl's fear, her courage it was undeniable. He stripped the man of his titles and exiled him from the kingdom. He also worked to heal the family, ensuring the girl had the support she needed.

That's powerful, Mrs. Love said, her eyes misty.

It wasn't always so clear, Ife added. There was another case, a young man who had been assaulted by his friend's uncle. The shame and fear he felt nearly consumed him. It took everything in my father's power to convince the boy to speak up. When he finally did, my father ensured the uncle faced justice. But it left scars on the boy, on his family, on all of us.

Jake clenched his fists. It sounds like your dad didn't back down from tough decisions. He didn't, Ife said firmly. He believed justice wasn't just about punishment it was about restoring balance and protecting the vulnerable. It's something I admired deeply about him. Later that evening, Ife sat with her mother, Mrs. Love, in the kitchen as they washed dishes. The rest of the family had gone to bed, and the house was quiet.

Mom, Ife said suddenly, did you know about the Rose of Venus?

Mrs. Love glanced at her, curious. What?

It's a geometric pattern created by the dance of Venus and Earth every eight years, Ife explained, her voice soft with wonder. On Venus, my mother used to tell me about it. She said each petal represents a stage on the pathway to greater love.

That's beautiful, Mrs. Love said, pausing to look at her daughter. "What do you think it means?

I think it's a reminder, Ife said, her gaze distant. That love isn't just a feeling. It's a journey. It's about growth, forgiveness, and understanding whether it's between two people, two families, or two worlds.

Mrs. Love smiled, placing a hand on her daughter's. That sounds like something you're learning here, too.

Ife met her eyes, a flicker of gratitude in her expression. I think so. I mean, I'm starting to make sense of it all. My memories of Venus, my life here as Iris it's like the petals of the rose, coming together to create something whole.

Mrs. Love squeezed her hand. You've always been whole, honey. It just takes time to see it. That night, Ife stood in her room, holding a photo of her Earth family. Memories of Venus swirled in her mind her father's justice, her mother's wisdom, her siblings' laughter. She thought of the feasts, the friendships, the struggles for harmony.

I'm the bridge, she whispered to herself, repeating the words of her Venusian mother. I'm meant to bring harmony, to connect what feels divided.

Her gaze shifted to her reflection in the mirror. For the first time, she saw herself clearly not just as Iris or Ife, but as both.

The journey wasn't over. There were still questions to answer, connections to mend, and truths to uncover. But as Ife lay down to sleep, she felt a deep sense of peace. She was exactly where she needed to be.

Ife sat cross legged on her bed, gazing out the window at the night sky. The soft glow of Venus twinkled faintly, almost as if calling to her. She closed her eyes, letting the quiet pull her into another memory.

She was back on Venus, standing in a golden forest. The air was warm, and the leaves shimmered like molten sunlight. Princess Lewa stood in front of her, her silver hair cascading over her shoulders, her emerald, green eyes filled with a mix of joy and nervousness.

Ife, Lewa whispered, her voice trembling slightly. You know this is dangerous.

I don't care, Ife replied, stepping closer. I love you, Lewa. I've loved you since the day we met.

Lewa's lips curved into a smile, her laughter soft and melodic. You're impossible, you know that? Only for you, Ife said, her voice tender. And then, without another word, Lewa leaned in, their lips meeting in a kiss that sent shivers down Ife's spine. It was sweet and electric, filled with the passion and fear of something forbidden.

When they finally pulled apart, Lewa's cheeks were flushed. If anyone finds out

They won't, Ife interrupted, her tone firm. We'll be careful. I'm not letting anyone, not even our families, take this away from us.

Lewa cupped Ife's face, her touch gentle. You're so brave. I wish I could be more like you.

You are brave, Ife said, holding her hand tightly. Brave enough to love me despite everything.

The memory shifted abruptly, and Ife found herself in the grand hall of the Taurean palace. The air was thick with tension, and the towering figure of Prince Ajaka loomed before her.

You can't avoid me forever, Ife, Ajaka said, his voice low but intense. His dark eyes bored into hers, his expression both longing and frustrated.

I'm not avoiding you, Ife replied, keeping her tone neutral. I've been busy.

With Lewa, no doubt, Ajaka said bitterly, his jaw tightening.

Ife's heart skipped a beat, but she forced herself to remain calm. She's my best friend. Of course, I spend time with her. Ajaka stepped closer, his gaze softening.

You don't have to pretend with me, Ife. I know how you look at her. But I also know there's something between us. There always has been.

Ajaka, I Ife began, but he cut her off.

Don't deny it, he said, his voice almost pleading. I see it in your eyes. You care for me.

Ife hesitated, guilt twisting in her chest. She did care for Ajaka, but not in the way he wanted.

I care about you, she said carefully. Your kind, loyal, and you've always been there for me. But... my heart belongs to someone else.

Ajaka's face darkened, and his hands clenched into fists. Lewa, he spat, his voice laced with anger. You love her.

Ajaka, please

No, he snapped, his voice rising. You don't understand what you're doing. If anyone finds out, it will destroy both of you. You'll shame your family and hers. Is that what you want?

Ife's throat tightened. I just want to be happy.

And I just want you, Ajaka said, his voice breaking. But it seems I'm the only one willing to do what it takes to protect you. Without another word, he turned and stormed out of the hall, leaving Ife alone with her racing thoughts. Ife opened her eyes, her heart pounding as the memory faded. She touched her lips, as if she could still feel the warmth of Lewa's kiss.

Her emotions were a storm love, regret, longing, and guilt all swirling within her. She glanced at the photo of her Earth family on the nightstand, feeling a pang of sadness.

Why am I remembering this now? she murmured to herself.

A knock at the door interrupted her thoughts. Come in, she called, her voice shaky.

Imani stepped inside, her expression concerned. You, okay? You look like you've seen a ghost.

I'm fine, Ife said quickly, though her trembling hands betrayed her. Just... remembering.

Imani sat beside her on the bed. Venus again?

Yes, Ife admitted. But this time, it's not just about the place. It's about someone I loved.

Imani raised an eyebrow. Loved?

Ife nodded. My friend Princess Lewa. She was everything to me. But our love was forbidden because of the rivalry between our families. And then there was Ajaka her brother. He was in love with me, and it made everything more complicated. Wow, Imani said, her eyes wide. That's... a lot. It was, Ife said, her voice heavy with emotion. But what hurts the most is not knowing what happened after. Did Lewa and I ever find peace? Did Ajaka forgive me? Or did it all fall apart because of the secrets and the rivalry?

Imani placed a hand on her sister's shoulder. You'll remember, Ife. It's all still inside you, waiting to come to the surface.

I hope so, Ife said quietly. Because I need to know if the love, I fought for was worth it.

A New Perspective

The morning sunlight spilled through the kitchen window, casting a warm glow over the table where Ife now slowly accepting her name as Iris sat with Mrs. Love.

Iris, her mother began cautiously, I know it's been a lot, balancing who you feel you are with the life you had here. But I want you to know that no matter what, we love you. Both as Iris and as Ife.

Iris smiled faintly, stirring her tea. Thanks, Mom. It's getting easier, I think. The memories from Venus they're not fading, but they don't feel as overwhelming anymore. And… I'm starting to see how the relationships I had there connect to the ones I have here.

Mrs. Love tilted her head curiously. How so?

Well, Iris began, on Venus, my relationship with Lewa was built on trust and love, even though it had to be hidden. And Ajaka… his feelings for me created so much tension. But when I look at the relationships I have here, I see echoes of that.

Mrs. Love's brow furrowed. In what way?

Imani reminds me of my sister, Lemanja, Iris explained. Always curious, always supportive. And Jake he has Baka's loyalty and protectiveness, even if he's a bit more laid back about it.

And me? Mrs. Love asked, her voice soft.

Iris reached out and placed her hand over her mother's. "You remind me of my mother on Venus. She was wise and nurturing, always guiding me, even when I didn't want to listen. But you're also different. You're... more present. More real.

Mrs. Love's eyes glistened with tears. I'm glad you feel that way, sweetheart. Because no matter where you come from or what you remember, this is your home too.

Later that afternoon, Jake found Iris sitting on the porch with Royal sprawled lazily at her feet.

Hey, sis, Jake said, flopping onto the porch swing beside her. You busy?

Not really, Iris replied, scratching Royal behind the ears. What's up?

I was thinking we could hang out today, Jake said. You know, just the two of us. There's this cool arcade downtown, and I thought maybe we could check it out. Iris raised an eyebrow. An arcade? Aren't you a little old for that?"

Jake smirked. Never too old for beating my sister at air hockey. Oh, you're on, Iris said, standing up and grabbing her jacket. At the arcade, laughter filled the air as

Jake and Iris battled it out at various games. By the time they reached the air hockey table, Iris was grinning from ear to ear.

You're going down, she said, grabbing the paddle.

Bring it, Jake shot back.

The game was intense, with both siblings shouting and laughing as the puck zoomed back and forth. When Iris scored the winning point, she threw her arms in the air triumphantly.

Victory! she exclaimed.

Alright, alright, Jake said, feigning defeat. You win this round. But next time, it's on.

As they walked out of the arcade, Iris turned to Jake. Thanks for today. I really needed this.

Jake slung an arm around her shoulders. Anytime, sis. You're stuck with me, after all.

That evening, Iris and Imani sat in the living room, flipping through an old photo album.

Look at this one! Imani said, pointing to a picture of a younger Iris covered in mud, holding up a frog.

Iris burst out laughing. What was I even doing?

You were trying to 'rescue' it from the puddle in the backyard, Imani said, giggling. You were so serious about it too. Kept saying, this frog has a destiny!

Iris shook her head, still laughing. I was such a dork.

Maybe, Imani said with a grin. But you were my dork. And you still are.

The laughter faded into a comfortable silence, and Iris flipped the page to a picture of the whole family at the beach.

I don't remember this day, she said softly.

Imani leaned closer. That was the summer before the accident. You and Jake built the biggest sandcastle I've ever seen. It even had a moat, and a little bridge made of driftwood.

Iris traced the edges of the photo with her finger. I wish I could remember it.

It's okay, Imani said, squeezing her hand. We'll make new memories. And who knows? Maybe bits and pieces of the old ones will come back when you least expect it.
Later that night, Iris found Mrs. Love in the kitchen, baking cookies. The warm, sugary scent filled the room as Iris sat at the counter.

Couldn't sleep? Mrs. Love asked without looking up.

Just thinking, Iris replied. Mrs. Love placed a tray of cookies in the oven and turned to her daughter. What's on your mind? I've been thinking about how lucky

I am to have all of you, Iris said, her voice soft. Even when I didn't remember you, you never gave up on me. That means more than I can put into words.

Mrs. Love smiled, coming around the counter to hug her tightly. That's what family does, Iris. We stick together, no matter what.

As Iris hugged her mother back, she felt a warmth she hadn't realized she was missing. For the first time, she felt truly at home not just on Earth, but in her heart.

It was family movie night at the Love household. The living room was cozy, filled with laughter as Iris, Imani, Jake, and their parents passed around bowls of popcorn. Royal lay curled up at Iris's feet, occasionally wagging his tail at the commotion.

Jake, I swear if you hog the popcorn one more time Imani warned, pointing a finger.

Relax, little sis, Jake teased, tossing a handful into his mouth.

Iris laughed, feeling a rare sense of peace. For the first time in weeks, the weight of her memories felt lighter.

But as the movie continued, a sudden wave of dizziness hit her. The room seemed to blur, and the voices of her family faded into the background.

Chapter Four: A Forbidden Love Revealed

In her mind, Iris was back on Venus. She stood in the royal garden, her breath hitching as Prince Ajaka confronted his mother, Empress Oduwa.

I've seen the way Lewa looks at her, Ajaka said, his voice sharp with anger. They're not just friends. There's something more.

Empress Oduwa's expression darkened, her lips tightening into a thin line. Are you certain, Ajaka?

Yes, he replied, his voice trembling. They're hiding it, but I've seen it. They sneak away during the feasts, and Lewa has been distant with me ever since Ife came into her life. I can't stand it.

Empress Oduwa's gaze hardened. "This cannot continue. Ife is a Libran, and Lewa is a Taurean princess. Their relationship would disgrace both families.

Ajaka stepped closer. You must do something, Mother. For the good of our family and for Lewa.

The memory shifted. Ife stood before her mother, Empress Ayao, who wore an expression of sorrow and resolve.

You cannot see Lewa again, Ayao said firmly.

What? Ife's voice cracked, her chest tightening. Why? What happened?

Empress Oduwa has forbidden her from seeing you, Ayao explained, her tone heavy with regret. She believes your relationship threatens the unity of the royal families.

And you agree with her? Ife demanded, her heart breaking.

Empress Ayao hesitated, then placed a hand on her daughter's shoulder. I do not. But as Empress, I must protect you and our family. If we defy Oduwa, it could lead to chaos.

Tears streamed down Ife's face as she shook her head. You don't understand. I love her.

Ayao's expression softened, but her voice remained firm. Love is not enough, my child. Sometimes, sacrifices must be made for the greater good.

Iris?

A voice broke through the haze, pulling her back to the present. She blinked, realizing Imani was kneeling in front of her, concern etched on her face.

Are you okay? Imani asked, gripping her hands.

I... I'm fine, Iris said, though her trembling voice betrayed her.

Jake leaned forward; his brows furrowed. You zoned out for a minute there. What happened?

Iris shook her head, struggling to find the words. Just... a memory.

Mrs. Love turned off the TV, her attention fully on Iris. Do you want to talk about it?

Iris hesitated, tears welling in her eyes. It's... hard. On Venus, I loved someone, Princess Lewa, but her family found out and forbade her from seeing me. Then my mother forbade me too. It was... devastating. I've never felt so helpless.

Imani squeezed her hands. That's horrible. I'm so sorry, Iris.

I think it's why I've never let myself get close to anyone here, Iris continued, her voice breaking. The pain of losing Lewa... it made me scared to love again.

Mrs. Love wrapped her arms around Iris, pulling her into a comforting embrace. Oh, sweetheart. I'm so sorry you had to go through that. But you're safe here. You're loved.

Jake leaned back, his expression thoughtful. You know, Iris, maybe this is why you're here. To heal from all of that. To learn that love doesn't have to end in pain.

Iris sniffled, managing a small smile. Maybe you're right. I just... I didn't expect it to hurt so much, even now.

That's because you loved her deeply, Mrs. Love said, stroking her hair. And that's not something to be ashamed of. But don't let the past stop you from finding happiness now.

The next morning, Iris woke feeling emotionally raw but lighter. She found Imani waiting for her in the kitchen, a steaming mug of coffee in hand.

I made you this, Imani said, sliding the mug toward her. Thought you could use it after last night.

Thanks, Iris said, smiling gratefully.

As they sipped their drinks in silence, Imani spoke. You know, it's okay to fear love after what you went through. But you've got us now. We're your family, and we're not going anywhere.

I know, Iris said, her voice steady. And that means everything to me. I don't think I could face these memories without you all.

Imani grinned. Good. Because you're stuck with us, whether you like it or not.

Iris laughed, the sound light and genuine. For the first time in what felt like forever, she felt hopeful not just for herself, but for the life she was rebuilding with her family.

Preparing for Visitors

The Love household buzzed with energy as Iris sat at the kitchen table, nervously tapping her fingers. Mrs. Love bustled around, setting out snacks, while Imani gave Royal a stern look as he tried to sneak a piece of bread from the counter.

They're just coworkers, Iris, Imani said, smirking. Why are you so jittery?

I don't know, Iris admitted. It feels strange. I haven't seen Ishara or Bryce since before the accident. I don't even know if I'll recognize them or remember what they mean to me.

Mrs. Love placed a reassuring hand on her shoulder. Just take it one step at a time. They're here because they care about you.

I hope so, Iris murmured, her thoughts flickering to Lewa and Ajaka. The memories of forbidden love and heartbreak still lingered, making her wonder if her Venusian past had somehow shaped her inability to form deeper connections on Earth.

Before she could spiral further, the doorbell rang, jolting her back to the present.

When Iris opened the door, two familiar faces greeted her. Ishara stood with a bouquet of flowers, her dark curls framing her kind, earnest face. Beside her, Bryce held a box of chocolates, his confident grin faltering slightly when he saw Iris's cautious expression.

Hi, Iris, Ishara said gently. It's so good to see you.

Yeah, Bryce added, his voice warm but tinged with nervousness. We've missed you at the clinic.

Iris hesitated, searching their faces. Something stirred in her memory a flash of laughter in the breakroom, the comfort of shared jokes during long shifts.

Ishara, she said slowly, then looked at Bryce. And Bryce. I remember you.

Relief washed over both, and Ishara smiled brightly. We were so worried. How have you been? It's been… a journey, Iris admitted, stepping aside to let them in. But I'm getting better, one day at a time. The three of them sat in the living room, Royal happily napping at Bryce's feet. Ishara and Bryce took turns updating Iris on the clinic how things had been running, funny stories about patients, and how much they'd missed her presence.

You always knew how to keep us sane during crazy shifts, Ishara said with a laugh.

And no one makes coffee runs like you. Bryce added, grinning.

Iris chuckled softly, the warmth of their camaraderie easing her nerves. I miss it, too. I don't know when I'll be ready to come back, though.

There's no rush, Ishara said, her voice gentle. We just wanted to see you and make sure you're okay. As the conversation flowed, Iris couldn't help but notice the subtle dynamic between Ishara and Bryce. Ishara's gaze lingered on her a little longer than necessary, her words filled with quiet affection. Bryce, on the other hand, leaned closer when he spoke, his playful demeanor masking something deeper.

The realization unsettled her, stirring memories of Ajaka's unspoken love and how it had complicated her relationship with Lewa.

Are you alright? Ishara asked, her brow furrowing in concern.

Iris blinked, realizing she had zoned out. Yeah, sorry. Just... tired.
Maybe we should head out, Bryce suggested, though his reluctance was clear.
No, Iris said quickly. Stay a little longer. I want to hear more about what I've missed. As the evening wore on, Mrs. Love called Bryce into the kitchen to help her with something, leaving Iris and Ishara alone in the living room. Ishara

hesitated before speaking. Iris, can I be honest with you? Of course, Iris said, sitting up straighter.

I was terrified when I heard about your accident, Ishara admitted, her voice trembling slightly. The thought of losing you... I didn't realize how much you meant to me until then.

Iris's heart clenched, memories of Lewa's soft confession echoing in her mind.

I'm not trying to pressure you, Ishara said quickly, her cheeks flushing. I just... needed to tell you. No matter what happens, I'm here for you. Always.

Iris swallowed hard, unsure how to respond. She cared about Ishara, but the weight of her past made it difficult to untangle her feelings.

Thank you, she said finally. That means a lot to me.

Later, Bryce found Iris sitting on the porch, gazing at the stars. He sat beside her, offering her a soft smile.

Mind if I join you? he asked.

Not at all, Iris replied.
They sat in comfortable silence for a moment before Bryce spoke. You know, I've been meaning to tell you something since before the accident.

Iris turned to him, her heart sinking slightly. I like you, Iris, Bryce said, his voice steady but vulnerable. I have for a while. And when you were gone... it made me realize how much I care about you.

Iris's breath caught, the echoes of Ajaka's confession ringing in her ears. Bryce...

You don't have to say anything, he added quickly. I just needed you to know. No matter what, I'm here. As a friend or whatever you need.

Thank you, Iris said softly. You've always been a good friend.

Bryce smiled faintly, though she could see the flicker of disappointment in his eyes.

That night, Iris lay in bed, staring at the ceiling. The confessions from Ishara and Bryce replayed in her mind, intertwining with memories of Lewa and Ajaka.

On Venus, love had been a source of joy but also pain and sacrifice. Here on Earth, it seemed no less complicated. But as she thought of Ishara's kindness and Bryce's unwavering support, she felt a spark of hope.

Maybe this time, she whispered to herself, I can get it right.
She wasn't sure what the future held, but for the first time in a long while, she felt ready to face it with her family, her friends, and the lessons she'd learned from both worlds guiding her.

A Night at the Movies

The soft glow of the theater screen lit up Iris's face as she sat between Ishara and Bryce, their laughter blending with the crowds as the movie played. It had been a fun night so far until now. I'll go get us more popcorn, Bryce offered, standing up and giving Iris a warm smile. Thanks, Bryce, she said, her eyes following him as he left.

As the door closed behind him, Ishara leaned closer, whispering, are you having a good time?

Iris nodded, her heart fluttering. Yeah, I am.

Their eyes met, and in the dim light, the world seemed to fade away. Before Iris could second guess herself, Ishara leaned in, and their lips met in a gentle, tender kiss.

The moment felt perfect until a sharp voice cut through the air.

So, this is why you won't date me? Bryce's angry tone shattered the quiet, drawing the attention of nearby moviegoers. Because you like Ishara more than me?

Iris pulled back, her face flushing with a mix of guilt and shock. Bryce, it's not like that Not like that? Bryce scoffed, his voice rising. I've been waiting, hoping, and now I see the truth. You just didn't want me because you're into her!
People around them began whispering, shifting uncomfortably in their seats. Ishara looked horrified, trying to calm him down. Bryce, please, we didn't mean for you to find out like this.

But Bryce wasn't listening. His eyes locked on Iris, the hurt and betrayal clear. Why couldn't you just tell me? Why string me along? I wasn't stringing you along! Iris protested, her voice trembling. I like you, Bryce, just not in that way. As

Bryce's rage echoed in the theater, Iris's mind was suddenly pulled into a memory from Venus.

She stood in the grand hall of the Libran palace, her sister Lemanja rushing in, her face pale with worry.

Ife, Lemanja whispered urgently, I need to talk to you.

What's wrong? Ife asked, concern flooding her voice.

It's about Lewa, Lemanja said, her voice trembling. Ajaka told his mother about you two. That's why you're forbidden to see each other.

Ife's heart sank. What? How do you know this?

I saw Lewa at the market, Lemanja explained. She pulled me into an alley so no one would see us talking. She misses you terribly, Ife. She told me how much she loves you and apologized for her brother's actions.
What actions? Ife asked, dread pooling in her stomach.
Lewa was caught leaving her palace one night to see you, Lemanja said, her voice heavy. Empress Oduwa was furious. She's sending Lewa to Mercury to live with her father, Emperor Olorun. She can't trust her to stay in the castle anymore.

Back to Reality

Iris! Ishara's voice broke through the memory, pulling her back to the present.

Iris blinked, her breathing shallow as she focused on Ishara's concerned face. Are you okay? Ishara asked gently. I... I'm fine, Iris lied, her hands trembling.

Where's Bryce? He left, Ishara said softly. He told me he hates me and that I shouldn't look his way at work.

Iris's chest tightened with guilt. I'm so sorry, Ishara. This is all my fault. I must fix this. I can't let it happen again.

Again? Ishara asked, confusion flickering in her eyes. What do you mean?

I'll explain later, Iris said hurriedly, grabbing her things. I need to go home. I'll call you.

Back at home, Iris paced her room, her mind racing. The parallels between Bryce's outburst and Ajaka's betrayal on Venus were too stark to ignore. The guilt, the pain it was all too familiar.

She sat on her bed, burying her face in her hands. Why does this keep happening? she whispered to herself.
A knock at the door startled her. Come in, she called, her voice muffled.

Imani peeked in, her expression full of concern. Hey, I heard what happened at the movies. Are you okay?

No, Iris admitted, tears brimming in her eyes. It's like I'm reliving my past on Venus all over again. Bryce's reaction, the way things ended with Lewa it's all so similar. I don't know how to deal with it.

Imani sat beside her, placing a comforting hand on her back. You're not alone, Iris. Whatever happened on Venus, we'll figure it out together. But you must give yourself a break. It's okay to feel overwhelmed. I just... I don't want to hurt anyone, Iris said, her voice breaking. I care about Ishara, but I didn't mean for Bryce to get hurt.

Sometimes, Imani said gently, people get hurt no matter what you do. But that doesn't mean you're responsible for their feelings. You can't control everything, Iris.

Iris nodded slowly, wiping her eyes. I just need to figure out how to move forward. Without repeating the mistakes of my past.

And you will, Imani said with a reassuring smile. One step at a time.

Chapter Five: The Next Day

At the clinic, Iris felt a knot of anxiety tighten in her chest as she walked through the doors. The familiar hum of activity filled the air, but her eyes searched for Bryce and Ishara.

Spotting Ishara at the front desk, Iris approached hesitantly. Hey.

Ishara looked up, her expression softening. Hey. Are you okay?

I'm getting there, Iris said, managing a small smile. Is Bryce here?

Ishara shook her head. He called in sick. I think he just needs some space.

I understand, Iris said quietly. But I'm going to talk to him. I need to make things right.

I'm here for you, Ishara said, reaching out to squeeze her hand.

Thanks, Iris said, feeling a flicker of warmth. I'll see you later.

Later that day, Iris sat in her car, parked outside Bryce's apartment building. Her heart pounded as she rehearsed what she wanted to say. Taking a deep breath, she stepped out and made her way to his door, hoping he would hear her out.

She knocked softly. After a long pause, the door opened, and Bryce stood there, his expression guarded. Iris, he said flatly.
Hey, she replied, her voice tentative. Can we talk?

Bryce hesitated, then stepped aside, letting her in. The tension in the room was palpable as they sat on opposite ends of the couch.

I'm sorry, Iris began, her eyes meeting his. For everything. I didn't mean to hurt you.

Bryce crossed his arms, his jaw tightening. Why didn't you just tell me, Iris? You could've saved us both a lot of pain.

I know, she admitted, her voice heavy with regret. I should've been honest sooner. I care about you, Bryce, but not in the way you deserve.

Bryce's gaze softened slightly. I just don't get it. We were good together, weren't we? At least as friends?

We were, Iris said, nodding. And I still want us to be. But I've been through so much on Venus and here. It's hard for me to open fully, especially when it comes to love.

Bryce ran a hand through his hair, sighing. I guess I just hoped we could've been more.

I'm sorry, Iris repeated. I never wanted to hurt you. You've always been a great friend, and I hope we can find a way back to that.

Bryce looked at her for a long moment before finally nodding. It's going to take time, but... I think we can get there.
Relief washed over Iris, and she offered a small, grateful smile. Thank you, Bryce.

A New Beginning with Ishara

In the following days, Iris found herself spending more time with Ishara. Their connection felt natural, yet different from anything Iris had experienced before. One evening, they decided to take a walk in the park, enjoying the quiet beauty of the setting sun.

As they strolled along the path, Ishara glanced at Iris, her expression thoughtful. So, how did things go with Bryce?

We talked, Iris said, exhaling softly. It wasn't easy, but I think we're on the path to rebuilding our friendship. He understands now.

I'm glad, Ishara said, her tone sincere. He's a good guy. I hated seeing him hurt.

I hated it too, Iris admitted, her voice tinged with sadness. But I couldn't keep lying to myself or to him.

They walked in silence for a few moments before Ishara spoke again. And what about us?

Iris stopped, turning to face her. I want to take things slow. My past... it's complicated. But I care about you, Ishara. A lot.

Ishara smiled, her eyes reflecting the warmth of the setting sun. I care about you too. And I'm willing to take it slow. Relief filled Iris, and she reached out, taking Ishara's hand. Thank you. For understanding. For being here.
Always, Ishara said softly, intertwining their fingers. We'll figure this out together. Over the next few weeks, Iris and Ishara grew closer, navigating their

budding relationship with care and understanding. They spent time talking about their dreams, fears, and the parts of their lives that shaped them.

One evening, as they sat on Iris's porch, Ishara asked, do you think you'll ever go back to Venus?

Iris thought for a moment before answering. I don't know. Part of me feels like I belong there, but another part feels at home here with you, with my family. Maybe I don't have to choose. Maybe I can be a bridge between both worlds.

Ishara nodded thoughtfully. Whatever you decide, I'll support you.

Thank you, Iris said, her heart swelling with gratitude. I've spent so much time running from my past, but with you, I feel like I can finally embrace both parts of myself.

Ishara smiled, leaning in to kiss her gently. You're amazing, Iris. And I'm honored to be part of your journey.

As they sat together under the stars, Iris felt a sense of peace she hadn't known in a long time. She was finally beginning to heal, to trust, and to love again both on Earth and in her heart.

Iris and Ishara sat on a blanket spread out under the stars, the soft glow of candlelight flickering between them. The quiet hum of the evening surrounded them, creating a peaceful cocoon. I've never felt this... connected to someone before, Iris admitted, her fingers tracing patterns on Ishara's hand. It's like you see me, all of me. And you're not afraid. Ishara smiled gently. There's nothing to fear, Iris. You're incredible, and I'm lucky to be by your side. I'm the lucky one,

Iris said, her eyes shining. You've helped me see that I can have both worlds. That I can be Ife and Iris. That love doesn't have to be painful.

Ishara leaned in, their foreheads touching. I'm here for all of it. Whatever you need, wherever this journey takes you.

As they kissed, the world seemed to fade away, leaving only the warmth of their connection. It was a love that bridged time, space, and identities rooted in trust, understanding, and hope.

In the days that followed, Iris found herself reflecting more deeply on her dual identity. The memories of Venus and her life on Earth no longer felt like two separate realities. They had begun to intertwine, forming a single, complicated truth.

One evening, standing by the window and gazing at the stars, a thought struck her with unexpected clarity. My name, she whispered, her voice trembling with emotion, Ife. It means love.
Imani, lounging nearby with a book, perked up. What was that, sis?

My name, Iris repeated, turning to face her sister. Ife means love. And that's what I've been searching for all this time understanding how love connects both my worlds.

Imani smiled warmly. That makes perfect sense. You've always been the heart of this family, Iris. And now, you're the bridge the connection between Earth and Venus. Iris nodded, a newfound sense of peace washing over her. I finally understand. My purpose isn't just to remember Venus. It's to bring harmony to both worlds. Love... love is the key.

A Day in the Park

It was a perfect day for a picnic. Iris, her family, and Ishara sat beneath the shade of an old oak tree, their laughter carrying on the gentle breeze. Plates of sandwiches, fresh fruit, and pastries were spread across the blanket, and even Bryce had joined them. The tension between him, Ishara, and Iris had eased over time, and today felt like a fresh start.

As they ate, the wind began to pick up, rustling the leaves above them. Bryce stood, shading his eyes against the sunlight as he looked toward the horizon.

Hey, he said, his voice tinged with confusion. What's that?
Everyone turned to look. A sleek, metallic object descended gracefully from the sky, shimmering in the light. The winds grew stronger as the craft landed in a nearby clearing, its polished surface reflecting the sun.
Iris's heart pounded as she stood, her breath catching in her throat. That's... Mercurian.

Her family exchanged uneasy glances, but Iris's focus remained on the craft. The hatch opened with a soft hiss, and a lone figure stepped out, their movements slow and deliberate.

As the winds died down, the figure approached, their silver hair catching the light. Iris's eyes filled with tears as recognition washed over her.

Lewa, she whispered, her voice trembling. The figure stepped closer, and as the distance between them faded, Iris could see her clearly. Princess Lewa stood before her, regal and beautiful, her eyes glistening with emotion. Ife, Lewa said softly, her voice carrying across the clearing. It's me.

Iris took a shaky step forward, her voice cracking. I probably look so different now, in this vessel...

You do, Lewa replied, smiling faintly. But I would know you anywhere. I've finally found you.

Found me? Iris asked, her voice barely audible.
Lewa nodded, her expression grave. I've come to take you home. It's urgent, Venus needs you. Iris blinked through her tears, confusion tightening in her chest. Why do I have to return? Lewa's voice wavered as fresh tears streamed down her face. For revenge, of course, she whispered. For getting me sent away, for killing your father... and most of all, for killing you.

Iris's breath caught, her entire body locking up as the words left Lewa's lips. Her voice came out in a stunned whisper, full of disbelief and horror.

Ajaka... killed my father? Killed me?

The words felt foreign in her mouth, like they didn't belong to her like they couldn't be true. But deep inside, something cracked, and the memories she didn't know she had trembled beneath the surface, ready to rise.

At that moment, Mrs. Love rushed to her side, placing a protective hand on her shoulder. Iris, is everything alright? Who is this?

Iris swallowed hard, her voice barely above a breath. This is Princess Lewa.

Mrs. Love eyed, Lewa warily. Nice to meet you, but what's this about someone killing my daughter?

Lewa's fierce expression softened slightly, but sorrow lingered in her gaze. No one here will harm her. But I'm sad to say that she... she did die. On Venus. Ife's breath hitched, her mind struggling to grasp the weight of Lewa's words. I... I died on Venus. Her voice was barely a whisper, laced with disbelief. I don't remember that.

Lewa stepped closer, her expression both gentle and resolute. I can help you remember what happened. Come, Ife.

As Ife hesitated, Lewa lifted her hand, and a soft glow radiated from her fingertip. Without another word, she pressed it gently against the center of Ife's forehead. A sudden wave of energy pulsed through Ife's body. Her eyes fluttered, her breath caught in her throat, and before she could resist, her knees buckled. She sank to the ground, her body limp yet weightless, as the memories of the day she died came rushing back sharp, vivid, and undeniable.

The Night of Betrayal

Ife saw herself back on Venus, lost in grief after hearing the news that Lewa had been sent to Mercury to live with her father, King Olorun. The days blurred into weeks, then months. Ife barely ate, surviving on soup and tea. Her once bright spirit had withered, and Empress Ayao was at a loss, unable to console her daughter.

One day, Ife wandered into the golden forest, tears streaming down her face as she whispered to the wind. Lewa... I miss you.

Her words hung in the air, but she wasn't alone. Prince Ajaka appeared from the shadows, his expression dark.

You need to stop this, Ife, he said sharply, grabbing her arm. Lewa is gone. She's never coming back.

Get your hands off me! Ife snapped, pulling away. She's gone because of *you*! You told your mother about us, you destroyed everything!

Ajaka's jaw clenched. I did what I had to do. I loved you, Ife. I still do. Ife laughed bitterly through her tears. Love? You don't know the meaning of the word. You've done nothing but ruin me. They argued until the sun dipped below the horizon, the golden forest now cloaked in darkness. Finally, Ajaka's tone softened. Let me take you to the castle. It's cold, and you're tired. I'll make you tea.

Ife hesitated before nodding. She hadn't slept in weeks, and the thought of tea brought a faint smile to her lips.

In Lewa's room, Ife's heart ached as she ran her fingers over her lost love's belongings. She opened the closet, and a small box tied with a blue ribbon fell to the floor.

Empress Oduwa entered, her voice quiet. That box was meant for you. Lewa planned to give it to you the night my guards caught her sneaking out.

Tears filled Ife's eyes as she opened the box. Inside was a letter:

Ife, my love, my angel from above. Your beauty shames the day star, making darkness light and my heart seven times brighter. You are my greatest joy, and for you, I will love until my last breath.

Ife whispered, And I will love you until my last breath. Ajaka lingered for a moment, watching as Ife's lips formed that one fragile word Lewa... His expression darkened, but he said nothing. Instead, he turned on his heel and returned to the kitchen, his movements slow and calculated.

Empress Oduwa stood by the window, her gaze distant as regret settled deep within her. She had thought sending Lewa away was the right choice, a way to restore peace to their fractured family. But now, seeing Ife so heartbroken, so lost, she felt the weight of that decision crushing her. She turned to Ife, her voice gentle yet urgent. Ife, my dear, I'll be right back. There's something I must take care of. She offered a reassuring smile. I just need to make an urgent call.

Ife, drained from the night's events, barely reacted, only managing a small nod.

Meanwhile, Prince Ajaka returned to Lewa's chambers, a fresh cup of tea in hand. He stepped forward, his expression once again painted with false warmth.

Here, Ife. Drink up. This will help you rest.

Ife hesitated for only a moment before lifting the cup to her lips. The warmth of the tea spread through her, but instead of comfort, a deep chill crept into her limbs. Her body grew heavy, her vision swimming.

She blinked up at Ajaka, confusion turning into fear. What... what did you do?

The warmth vanished from Ajaka's face, replaced by something cold and unreadable. His voice, once soft, now cut like ice.

You were supposed to love me.

Ife's breath hitched, her heart pounding as her limbs weakened further. The world around her blurred, her body betraying her. Ajaka's expression twisted into something cruel. If I can't have you, no one will. Ife's tears fell freely, her lips parting in a final whisper. Lewa... And then, the world went dark. Ife came to with a sharp gasp, a scream tearing from her throat as tears streamed down her face. Her chest heaved, the lingering echoes of her final moments on Venus still gripping her. Before she could fully process where she was, warm arms wrapped around her. Shh, my love, you're safe. Ishara's voice was soft, soothing, as she pressed a gentle kiss to Ife's cheek. Everything is okay. You're here with us.

Lewa stood nearby, watching with glistening eyes as Ishara held Ife close, but she held back her own tears.

Ife's breaths slowed as she took in the familiar faces around her, her family, the people who had been her anchor in this life. But deep inside, she knew.

She slowly pulled away from Ishara and rose to her feet. Turning to her family, her voice was steady despite the weight of her decision.

I must return to Venus.

Mr. and Mrs. Love exchanged a look of understanding. They had always known this moment would come. Mrs. Love stepped forward, cupping Ife's face briefly before nodding. Be safe, sweetheart.

Mr. Love placed a reassuring hand on her shoulder. We'll always be here if you need us.

Ife turned to Imani and Jake, pulling them both into a tight hug.

Take care of each other, she murmured.

Jake smirked, though his voice was thick with emotion. You know we got this.

Imani swallowed hard, squeezing Ife's hand. Don't forget us.

Before Ife could respond, Bryce stepped forward, his usually confident demeanor faltering. Yeah... don't forget us. A soft smile touched Ife's lips. I won't. She glanced around one last time, memorizing every face, every emotion, before stepping back toward her destiny.

Before she could leave, Ishara gently cupped her face, their foreheads touching. Come back to me, she whispered.

Ife smiled, her heart aching and full all at once. I will, my love.

With that, she gave Ishara one last lingering kiss before turning to Lewa. Without another word, the two of them stepped forward, leaving the life Ife had known behind ready to reclaim the one that awaited her.

Chapter Six: Awakening the Bridge

When Ife stepped onto the Mercurian spacecraft, the sight before her took her breath away. Lewa's guards immediately knelt, their voices echoing in unison, Welcome, Princess Ife.

Ife stood frozen for a moment, unsure how to respond, before she heard Lewa's voice cut through the moment.

Captain, set the course for Mercury, Lewa commanded firmly.

Ife furrowed her brow in confusion. I thought we were going to Venus.

Not yet, Lewa replied, her tone softening. Our mothers, along with your brother and sister, are waiting for us there. But there's something we need to do on Mercury first.

Ife nodded slowly, still trying to process everything. Then Lewa's voice broke the silence again.

Let me ask you something, Ife.

Sure, go ahead, Ife said, her curiosity piqued.

How is it that you remember me? Lewa asked, her gaze steady and curious. You're not supposed to remember another life while living a new one. That's not how it works. Ife paused, her heart heavy with the memories of Earth. Well, I was in a car crash back on Earth. When I woke up, I couldn't remember who I was anymore. My memories of being Iris were gone, but... my life as Ife on Venus came back to me instead. And then, as I slowly regained my memories as Iris, my memories of Venus never faded. They stayed with me, like two lives running in parallel.

Lewa's eyes widened slightly, her voice filled with wonder. That's incredible. It's so rare to remember both worlds like that.

Ife gave a small smile. Yeah, it's wild.

For a moment, silence filled the cabin, and Ife noticed Lewa's eyes lingering on her.

Why are you staring at me like that? Ife asked, a faint blush rising to her cheeks.

Lewa tilted her head slightly, her lips curving into a soft smile. Your new vessel it's so beautiful. But then again, your energy has always been divine.

Ife felt her cheeks burn as Lewa's words settled over her, her voice carrying the same tenderness Ife remembered from a lifetime ago.

The two sat in comfortable silence for a moment before Ife's voice broke through. I'm so nervous, she admitted, her voice trembling slightly. It's been a lifetime since I've seen my family. I can't believe they're still alive. But my father... I'm still so angry about what happened to him.

Lewa placed a gentle hand on Ife's shoulder. Maybe, when this is all over, we can try to find him. Remember, energy doesn't die. You're right, Ife said softly, her voice laced with pain. But what if he doesn't have any memories of us? I don't want to disrupt his life, wherever he is. Yeah, you're probably right, Lewa agreed with a small nod. But... it wasn't by accident that you were in that car crash. The universe knew you had to remember me so you could come back home. Still, it wouldn't hurt to check in on him just to see how he's doing, wherever he might be.

Ife thought for a moment before nodding. You're right. It won't hurt. But once this is done, I'm going back to Earth, Lewa.

Lewa's head snapped up, her eyes narrowing. Why?

To be with Ishara or whatever her name is? Lewa's voice cracked slightly, the hurt creeping through.

No, Ife said quickly, though her tone was sharp. Because that's my family, Lewa. I have a whole life there.

Lewa crossed her arms, her tone turning bitter. Yeah, but you remembered your real family for a reason. What about them? What about me? You were stolen from us, Ife. Stolen. And you're just going to leave right after we deal with Ajaka? Her voice broke, tears streaming down her face. I can't believe you.

Ife's chest tightened, torn between two worlds and two loves. She didn't know what she was going to do, but she couldn't deny the deep ache to see her family again. Would they even recognize me? Would they accept me now that I looked so different? As Lewa wiped her tears and turned away, Ife stared out the window of the spacecraft, the stars rushing past like her thoughts fast, chaotic, and full of questions she wasn't ready to answer. As they entered Mercury's atmosphere, the view outside the spacecraft was breathtaking. Ife's eyes widened, her breath catching as she took in the sight. The planet shimmered in shades of gold and silver, its surface reflecting the light of nearby stars. The landscape below was dotted with towering crystalline structures and lush, glowing fields.

I can't believe how beautiful it is, Ife whispered to herself, her fingers brushing the glass as she leaned closer.

Lewa, seated beside her, glanced over. She couldn't help but smile at the wonder lighting up Ife's face. Seeing her smile again filled Lewa with a quiet sense of relief. She hadn't meant to upset Ife earlier she could only imagine how overwhelming this all must be for her. Still, as Lewa watched her, one thought kept repeating in her mind, *Ife truly is the bridge for both worlds.*

As they neared the landing site, Ife's stomach tightened with nerves. Each passing moment brought her closer to seeing her mother, brother, and sister, family she hadn't seen in centuries.

When the craft finally touched down, Ife's heart raced. She peered out the window and saw her mother, Empress Ayao, waiting just outside, her hands clasped tightly as if to steady herself. The welcoming party must have been alerted to their arrival.
Lewa reached over and gently took Ife's hands in hers. Are you ready for this reunion? she asked softly. Ife swallowed hard. No. And yes. But what choice do I have? Lewa squeezed her hands with a reassuring smile as the craft's hatch opened, allowing the warm, golden light of Mercury to flood the cabin.

The moment Ife stepped onto the ground, Empress Ayao ran toward her, tears streaming down her face. Mom, Ife said, her voice trembling. Yes, my dear. It's me, Empress Ayao said, pulling her into a tight embrace. You recognize me? Of course, Ife said, her voice breaking. You look the same mom, just older that's all.

Empress Ayao stepped back just enough to hold Ife's face in her hands, her tears falling freely. And you, my child. You're in a new vessel, yes, but your essence, your energy, is unmistakable. Here, look. She pulled a small photograph from her robes and handed it to Ife.

The picture showed Ife in her old Venusian vessel, in her original form. Ife studied the image, her heart swelling with emotion. I can see the similarities, she said, her voice barely above a whisper. Even in a different vessel, I don't look too different... but different enough.

Empress Ayao pulled her into another embrace, unable to stop hugging her daughter. Nearby, Empress Oduwa greeted her own daughter with a warm embrace. Welcome, my child, Empress Oduwa said softly. How was your trip? And... what was it like seeing Princess Ife again? Lewa sighed dramatically, rolling her eyes. She fell in love with a human, Mom. A human. Empress Oduwa chuckled, her tone gentle. Well, she *is* human now, my dear. And yet, you love her just the same.

Lewa's shoulders softened, and a small smile played on her lips. Yeah. Because I know who she truly is. She's Venusian through and through.

Suddenly, Ife's siblings, Princess Lemanja and Prince Baka, came rushing forward. Lemanja's laughter rang out as she threw her arms around Ife. Sister! she exclaimed.

Ife froze for a moment, shocked to see her once younger siblings now fully grown. Tears welled in her eyes as she hugged them tightly. You're all grown up, she whispered, her voice shaking. You're adults now. She pulled back, taking in

Baka's tall, imposing frame. Look at you, Prince Baka. All big and strong, just like Dad.

Baka smiled warmly. It's Emperor Baka now, he corrected gently. I've married and had children of my own.

Tears spilled down Ife's cheeks as she stared at him, her voice trembling with joy. I'm... I'm an aunt?

Baka nodded, turning to gesture behind him. Yes. This is my wife, Indragni, and my daughter, Sakhra.

Ife immediately embraced them, her heart overwhelmed. It's a pleasure to meet you both, she said, her voice filled with sincerity. Indragni smiled, her tone equally warm. No, the pleasure is all ours. This is such an amazing moment to witness a family reunion like this. Baka has spoken of you endlessly, about how beautiful and kind his big sister was. And now, here you are, returned to us from another world. It's truly a blissing.

Ife wiped her tears and pulled them all into another embrace, overwhelmed by the love and joy surrounding her. For the first time in centuries, she felt like she had truly come home.

Later that evening, Empress Oduwa was in the kitchen, her hands busy preparing a grand Taurean feast. Beside her, Empress Ayao worked with the same determination, their movements synchronized as if no time had passed since they were children. The two empresses laughed softly as they reminisced, but their shared goal was clear, they were determined to right the wrongs of their fathers, who had once ruled Venus and sowed discord between their families. Meanwhile, in the war room, Baka was showing Ife the military's plans and the strategic action they would take once they returned to Venus. Maps of Venusian territories lay spread across the table, and holograms of battalions shimmered above the surface.

You've got a sharp mind, Baka said, gesturing to the plans. But for all of this to work, I need to know something important.

What's that? Ife asked, tilting her head curiously.

Are you ready for your powers? Baka asked bluntly, his eyes narrowing with seriousness. Ife blinked in confusion. Powers? What powers? Baka glanced at Lewa, raising an eyebrow. I thought you'd awakened her fully by now. Lewa shook her head, her expression defensive. No, I haven't. Everything has been overwhelming for her, and I didn't want to throw everything at her all at once. She already had so much to process her memories of us, your father's death, and leaving Earth. Her voice softened. I didn't think she was ready.

Baka nodded, his expression softening with understanding. Fair enough. But now's the time. Ife needs to be strong for what's ahead.

At that moment, Empress Ayao entered the room, her presence commanding yet gentle. I can restore her royal essence, she said, her voice calm but resolute. She turned to Lewa, her tone polite but firm. With your permission, Princess Lewa?

Of course, Lewa replied with a slight bow. It would be my pleasure.

Empress Ayao walked toward Ife, extending her glowing hands. Come to me, my daughter, she said warmly. Close your eyes and trust me. Ife hesitated for a moment but then stepped forward, closing her eyes as instructed. She took a deep breath, and Empress Ayao's hands lit up with radiant energy. Placing her hands gently on her crown, the Empress murmured ancient words of power. The room seemed to hum with energy as Ife's body began to glow, her Libran symbol appearing on her forehead. Slowly, she began to levitate, her body suspended in midair as the energy of her royal essence returned to her.

When the ritual was complete, Ife gasped, startled by the sensations coursing through her body. She fell to the ground, her breathing heavy, her heart racing.

Baka knelt beside her, offering a reassuring smile. No worries, big sister. You'll get the hang of it. I'll train you myself to master your powers and to control them. Ife looked up at him, her voice shaky. I had no idea I could... do that. Baka smirked. Somebody was supposed to start training you on the way here, he teased, shooting a playful look at Lewa.

Lewa rolled her eyes. Yes, because I wasn't busy dealing with everything else that happened, right?

Enough, Empress Oduwa called out from the kitchen doorway, her voice light. The food is ready.

At those words, everyone's focus shifted. The room erupted with excitement as they rushed toward the dining area.

The dining table was packed with more food than Ife had seen in centuries. Every dish seemed to sparkle with the rich colors of Taurean tradition golden fruits, vibrant stews, and glimmering platters of roasted delicacies. It's just like I remember, Ife said softly, her heart swelling with nostalgia. As they ate, Ife's gaze drifted to Empress Oduwa and Emperor Olorun, seated together at the far end of the table. She turned to Lewa. Did your parents get back together?

Lewa nodded. Yes.

That's amazing, Ife said, smiling. What ever happened to them? How did your father end up on Mercury?

Lewa leaned back in her chair, taking a sip of her drink before answering. Long story short, Mercury was preparing for war with the Martians, and they called my dad for help. He took a small group of soldiers with him, and the battle lasted for centuries. While he was there, he fell in love with a Mercurian woman. They married, but about a century ago, she passed away. They didn't have any children.

I'm so sorry, Ife said softly.

Lewa shrugged. It's alright. I hadn't seen him since we were kids until my mother sent me to live with him. But after everything that happened with Ajaka, my parents have gotten close again. He's planning to come back home.

That's amazing, Ife said, nodding. I can understand it, though.

Lewa gave her a knowing look. I bet you do, falling in love with a human and all.

Ife ignored the comment, redirecting the conversation. So why did everyone come here to Mercury instead of staying on Venus? Lewa sighed. Our mothers were defenseless. Ajaka had just killed your father in battle and most of the guards abandoned them and joined Ajaka's side. One of his soldiers secretly warned my mother that we needed to flee because Ajaka planned to take over Empress Ayao's castle next. My father sent for us, to come to Mercury, for safety.

Sounds about right, Ife said, shaking her head. Thanks for breaking it down. For the next several months, Ife trained harder than she ever had in her life. Under Baka's guidance, she relearned how to fly, mastering the art of levitation with ease. She honed her healing abilities, channeling her energy to restore life to the most barren plants in Mercury's gardens. She practiced controlling the weather, summoning winds and storms with the flick of her hand.

She even learned how to fire laser beams from her palms, a skill she'd forgotten entirely but quickly mastered again. With every success, her confidence grew, and her mother's pride swelled.

One evening, Empress Ayao stood in the training grounds, watching Ife spar with Lewa in the golden glow of Mercury's twin moons. She whispered to herself, her voice filled with hope.

She truly is the bridge. Venus will be saved.

Chapter Seven: Eclipsed Hearts

The return to Venus was only two days away. Ife had sought peace in the Mercury Golden Garden, a place where the golden leaves shimmered like stars under the light of the twin suns. She sat cross legged on a smooth crystal stone, her breathing steady, her energy calm as she meditated.

But her tranquility was broken when Lewa appeared, her steps soft but her words sharp. Are you in love with her?

Ife's focus shattered, and she opened her eyes, irritation flashing across her face. We are two days away from going back to Venus to a war with your brother, she snapped.

Your brother, Lewa. We might have to take his life if he doesn't surrender. And yet, all you can think about is my love for Ishara?
Why does that concern you?

Lewa's mouth opened as if to respond, but she froze, stunned by Ife's sudden outburst.

What don't you get? Ife cut her off, her voice rising. I was killed, Lewa. I died. Then I was born into a new world where I became human. I built an entirely new life there, family, friends, and yes, love interests. She paused, her voice trembling with anger. I didn't even know you existed until my accident on Earth. You like to call it fate? I call it a curse. I'm living with two sets of memories, two completely different lives, two families I love more than anything, two worlds pulling me apart, and two lovers. How do you think that feels? Ife stood, her energy radiating off her in waves as her frustration peaked. And in case you didn't notice, she said coldly, I'm human now. I may have Venusian powers and my memories, but I'm not the person you lost centuries ago. I wouldn't let anyone disrespect you, and I'm damn sure not going to let you disrespect Ishara no matter what you think of humans.

Before Lewa could respond, Ife stormed off, her emotions raw and her patience exhausted. She headed back to the palace, leaving Lewa standing alone among the golden trees.

Later that evening, Lewa walked quietly into Ife's room. The air was still, the soft glow of the moonlight spilling through the windows and casting shadows on Ife's sleeping form.

Lewa hesitated for a moment, unsure whether to wake her.

But as she watched Ife, she felt the weight of her emotions pressing against her chest. She couldn't hold it in anymore. Taking a breath, she began speaking softly, unaware that Ife had opened her eyes the moment she heard the door.

I'm sorry, Lewa began, her voice trembling slightly. I'm sorry for how I've treated Ishara. I know you had an entire life there, and you didn't even know who I was until the accident. I understand that now.

It's just... I've spent centuries searching for you, Ife. When you died, I was shattered. I couldn't eat, I couldn't sleep, I was completely lost. She swallowed hard, her eyes glistening with emotion. I would rather lose you to another than have you be upset with me. Lewa moved closer, and Ife kissed her gently at first, then with a growing intensity that made Lewa's knees weak. When they pulled back, Lewa stared into her eyes, her voice barely above a whisper. I've been wanting to do that ever since I found you.

So why didn't you? Ife teased softly.

Lewa smiled, brushing her fingers against Ife's cheek. Because someone beat me to the punch.

They both laughed, the tension between them finally easing. Lewa's hands trailed down to Ife's shoulders, and her voice turned gentle. You need more rest. Tomorrow will be another long day.

Don't leave, Ife said, her voice soft but insistent. I want you here.

Lewa hesitated for only a moment before stepping closer. Ife stood, her heart pounding as she pulled Lewa into another kiss. This time, it was deeper, their breaths mingling as Ife's lips trailed from Lewa's mouth to her neck, leaving a trail of warmth.

Lewa stopped her, holding her gaze steady. She reached for the hem of her clothing, sliding it off effortlessly, revealing her bare, glowing skin. The light of Venus shimmered off her, accentuating her natural radiance.

Follow me, Lewa said softly, her voice low and inviting.

Ife's breath hitched as she watched Lewa disappear into the adjoining bathroom. Steam began to fill the air, curling out from the door as the sound of running water echoed in the room. Ife followed, her heart racing. Inside, the shower was already running, warm streams cascading down like liquid gold. Lewa stood beneath the water, her head tilted back, droplets clinging to her shimmering skin. She turned to Ife, her expression a mixture of love and desire.

Without hesitation, Ife stepped forward, letting her own clothes fall to the ground. The warmth of the water enveloped her as she joined Lewa, their bodies inches apart.

Lewa reached for Ife, her hands tracing the curves of her shoulders and arms, her touch both tender and electrifying. You're even more beautiful than I remember, Lewa murmured, her voice husky.

Ife's lips quirked into a small smile. And you're as breathtaking as ever.

Their lips met again, this time with an intensity that left no room for hesitation. The water streamed around them, blending the heat of their bodies with the steam that filled the room. Lewa's hands explored Ife's body, her touch sending waves of warmth through her.

Ife pressed Lewa against the cool tile, her lips moving down her neck, tasting the salt of her skin mixed with the sweet warmth of the water. Lewa let out a soft gasp, her fingers tangling in Ife's hair.

They moved in perfect harmony, the passion between them igniting like a fire that refused to be extinguished. Time seemed to stand still as they explored one another, their connection deeper than just the physical it was cosmic, timeless, unshaken by centuries or distance. When they finally pulled apart, their foreheads rested together, their breathing heavy. Lewa's lips curved into a small smile as she whispered, you are mine, Ife. And you are mine, Ife replied, her voice steady, her heart full.

They stayed like that for a while, the water washing away everything but the love and desire they shared, preparing them for the battles that lay ahead.

The Calm Before the Storm

The rising sun on Mercury rose high, bathing the golden palace in a soft glow. The twin suns cast a warm light through the crystalline windows of Ife's room, where she lay awake in bed. Her thoughts were heavy with the events of the previous night the tenderness she shared with Lewa, the weight of their love, and the daunting reality of their impending return to Venus.

She turned her head to find Lewa already awake, sitting by the window. Lewa was deep in thought, her gaze fixed on the distant horizon of Mercury's golden gardens. Her usually composed demeanor seemed cracked, her emotions leaking through the mask of regal calm she always wore.

Ife sat up, the sheets slipping from her shoulders. Lewa?

Lewa turned to her, a faint smile tugging at her lips. Good rising, my love.

Rising, Ife said softly, crossing the room to join her by the window. She placed a hand on Lewa's shoulder, squeezing gently. You seem troubled. Lewa let out a long sigh. I'm just... thinking about what's coming. Venus, Ajaka, the war. There's so much at stake. She paused before adding, And I can't stop thinking about how much I could lose. You, my family, our world... everything. Ife frowned, her heart aching for Lewa. She leaned down, pressing a kiss to her temple. We'll face it together. No matter what happens, you won't lose me. I promise.

Lewa closed her eyes, leaning into the touch. I believe you, Ife. And that's the only thing giving me strength right now.

By midday, the entire palace was alive with movement. Soldiers sparred in the training grounds, strategists pored over maps, and the air buzzed with tension.

Ife met with Baka in the war room. He stood at the center of the room, pointing at a massive holographic map of Venus that floated above the table. Lewa and Ayao were already there, listening intently.

Ife, Baka said as she entered, his tone commanding but warm. We need to review your role in the battle.

My role? Ife asked, raising an eyebrow.

Yes, Baka replied. You're the bridge between Earth and Venus. That's not just symbolic it's literal. Your powers will be instrumental in this fight. You'll lead the charge against Ajaka's forces.

Ife's heart skipped a beat. Lead? Baka, I barely relearned my powers.

Baka's face softened, and he placed a hand on her shoulder. You've trained harder than anyone, and you've mastered your abilities faster than I could've imagined. You're ready. Empress Ayao stepped forward, her voice calm but firm. Your role isn't just about fighting, Ife. It's about showing the people of Venus that there's hope. That unity is possible. You're the symbol they need. Ife nodded slowly, the weight of her responsibility settling on her shoulders. I understand.

Later in the afternoon, Ife joined Baka in the training grounds for her final session. The golden sands of Mercury sparkled under the light of the twin suns as Baka stood opposite her, his expression serious.

Today, we push you to your limits, Baka said. I need to know you're ready for anything Ajaka throws at us.

Ife squared her shoulders. I'm ready.

Baka raised his hand, summoning a massive wave of golden energy that surged toward her. Ife closed her eyes, her instincts kicking in. She raised her hands, summoning a barrier of wind that deflected the energy.

Good, Baka said, nodding. But don't just defend strike back!

Ife focused her energy, her palms glowing with white hot light. She released a beam of energy that shot toward Baka, who dodged with ease.

You can do better than that, Baka taunted playfully.

Ife smirked, her confidence growing. She summoned a storm of wind and lightning, her powers surging as the elements bent to her will. The ground beneath her cracked, and the air buzzed with raw energy. Baka raised his hands in surrender, laughing. Alright, alright! I yield! The two siblings burst into laughter, the tension easing for a moment. You've come a long way, Ife, Baka said, pride evident in his voice. You're ready.

An Evening of Reflection

As the day ended, the palace quieted. The weight of the upcoming battle hung heavily in the air, but for the moment, there was peace.

Ife found herself back in the golden garden, gazing up at the twin moons of Mercury. Lewa joined her, sitting beside her on the cool grass.

Do you think we can win? Lewa asked softly, her voice barely audible over the rustling leaves.

I think we must, Ife replied. For Venus. For everyone who's counting on us.

Lewa reached for Ife's hand, intertwining their fingers. And for us, she added.

Ife turned to her, her eyes soft. And for us, she agreed.

They sat in silence for a while, the stars above them shimmering like a thousand tiny promises.

As the Mercury sun rose, its golden light spilling over the palace, Emperor Baka stood in his chambers, preparing for the day ahead. His wife, Empress Indragni, stirred beside him, her gaze soft as she watched him dress in his battle armor. He leaned over, cupping her face gently as he kissed her lips.

I love you, my dearest, Baka whispered. And I love you, Indragni replied, her voice trembling ever so slightly. Baka turned to see their daughter, Princess Sakhra, standing at the door, her tiny frame bathed in the rising light. She ran to him, clutching his leg tightly. Daddy, why can't we go back home with you and Grandma?

Baka knelt, looking into her wide, innocent eyes. He placed a soft kiss on her forehead. My daughter, it would be too dangerous. But don't worry. Once everything is restored, I will send word for you and your mother to return home safely.

She nodded reluctantly, her lips quivering. Okay, Daddy. I love you.

And I love you, my precious star, Baka said warmly. He stood and turned back to Indragni, his eyes filled with a love so deep it anchored him. And I love you most of all.

Indragni smiled through her tears. And I love you, my love. Return to us safely.

Baka pulled them both into one last embrace before standing tall, his expression resolute. He left the chambers and made his way to the palace courtyard, where Ife and the rest of the family were waiting.

As he approached, Ife turned to him, her eyes briefly catching the shining light. She studied her brother, who resembled their father so strongly in his posture, his features, and his commanding presence.

Dad would love this, she said softly. Baka nodded, a faint smile touching his lips. Yes, he would. He'd be proud to see us fighting to restore what he once stood for. Ife sighed, glancing around. Wait... where's Lemanja? She's staying back, Baka explained. She'll remain here with Indragni and Sakhra to protect them if anything happens. Ife nodded. Understood. The family exchanged brief but meaningful glances before boarding the spacecraft. Once inside, Baka spoke firmly to the captain. Stay the course. We're heading home.

Chapter Eight: Entering Venus's Atmosphere

As the ship breached Venus's atmosphere, the breathtaking sight brought a wave of emotions crashing over Ife. The planet was as stunning as she remembered its golden skies swirling with soft hues of purple and silver, the lush landscapes glowing with vibrant life.

Ife leaned against the glass, her eyes brimming with nostalgia and disbelief.

What are you thinking? Lewa asked, standing beside her.

Ife shook her head, a faint smile on her lips. I'm surprised to see it still standing, to be honest. With Ajaka running things, I expected everything to be in ruins.

Lewa chuckled, and even the others in the cabin couldn't help but laugh.

Emperor Olorun's deep voice cut through the moment. When we arrive, I will speak with Ajaka. If he refuses to reason… He paused, his jaw tightening. Then I will do what must be done.

Lewa's face hardened. Go against your own son?

Emperor Olorun nodded solemnly. If that is what it takes to restore order, then yes.

As the ship descended into the golden forest near Lewa's castle, its secure location ensured they wouldn't be spotted by Ajaka's forces immediately. Ife's heart pounded as she stepped off the craft, the familiar scents of Venus filling her lungs.

Lewa reached for her hand, squeezing it gently. Are you ready for this, my love?

Ife hesitated before exhaling deeply. I'm as ready as I'll ever be.

Emperor Olorun, Lewa, and Ife made their way toward the castle while the rest of the family and their army of one hundred and forty-four thousand soldiers remained hidden in the forest, awaiting their signal.

The guards stationed at the castle gates immediately recognized Emperor Olorun. They exchanged uncertain glances before kneeling and stepping aside, allowing them entry.

As the three entered the grand hall, Ajaka's eyes widened at the sight of his father and sister. His gaze lingered on Ife, confusion flickering across his face as he studied her.

Father. Lewa. Ajaka's voice was sharp, his surprise quickly morphing into suspicion. What are you doing here? His eyes darted to Ife, narrowing. And who is this stranger? He hesitated, then added, her energy... it feels familiar.

Emperor Olorun stepped forward, his voice calm but commanding. I have returned home, Ajaka. I am here to restore our world to what it once was before your grandfather and Ife's grandfather turned it into a battleground. Ajaka's face twisted with disdain. Ife? She's gone. Ife stepped forward, her voice steady and sharp. Really, Ajaka? You don't recognize the love of your life? The one you killed that night with your poisoned tea. Ajaka's expression faltered, his bravado slipping as shock took over. No... no way. How can this be? How are you here?

Ife smirked, her eyes narrowing. Because I'm the bridge, Ajaka. The bridge between two worlds.

Ajaka's lips curled into a bitter smile. So, what's this, then? You've all come for revenge? And you, Father, you want me to step down from my throne, is that it?

Emperor Olorun nodded solemnly. It's the only way forward, son. You've brought nothing but chaos to this world.

Ajaka scoffed, his eyes flashing with anger. I'm not going anywhere. In fact, I consider it a reward that I get to kill Ife *twice*. He sneered at his father. And you were never there for me anyway. You want to lecture me now?

Ajaka, please, Olorun said, his tone pleading. Don't make me do this.

Do what, Father? Ajaka spat. Fight me? Go ahead. I've been waiting for this moment my entire life.

Before Emperor Olorun could respond, Ajaka's eyes flicked to the guards. Seize them! he barked.

At that moment, Emperor Olorun sent a telepathic signal to the ship, alerting the others to prepare for battle. Ife stepped forward, her energy pulsating with a calm yet formidable strength. She locked eyes with Ajaka, her voice unwavering. Don't worry you won't have the pleasure of killing me again. Ajaka's lips twisted into a bitter smirk. All you had to do was love me, Ife. That's all I ever wanted. But no, you were too busy being head over heels for Lewa.

Ife's brows furrowed, her expression a mix of pity and frustration. Ajaka, it's been centuries. I've been reborn on another planet, lived an entire human life, and grown into adulthood. You mean to tell me you're still harboring feelings for me after all this time? That's not love, it's madness.

Ajaka's face darkened, his jaw clenching.

If you stop this now, I will spare you, Ife said, her tone firm but offering one last chance. I'll even forgive you for killing my father.

Ajaka scoffed, his eyes narrowing. Your father fought well, I'll admit. But not well enough. That's war, Ife. Surely you understand.

Ife's heart burned with anger, but she remained composed. Yes, I understand war. And I understand what it means to end it.

Ajaka's laughter filled the hall, echoing off the high ceilings. End it? You? You're just a ghost of the past. Let's see if you can back up all this talk.

At that moment, the doors of the grand hall burst open. The ground beneath their feet rumbled as the one hundred and forty-four thousand soldiers charged through, led by Baka and Ayao. Stand down, Ajaka! Olorun commanded, his voice booming with authority. But Ajaka only sneered. Guards! Defend the castle!

Chapter Nine: The Battle Begins

Chaos erupted as the two armies clashed. The once grand halls of the castle were filled with the sound of swords clashing, energy blasts erupting, and battle cries echoing into the air.

Ife moved swiftly through the chaos, her powers igniting as her Libran symbol glowed fiercely on her forehead. She deflected attacks with barriers of wind and fired precise beams of energy from her palms, incapacitating Ajaka's guards with ease.

Nearby, Lewa fought with precision and ferocity, her twin daggers slicing through enemy ranks. Her movements were fluid, like a dancer on the battlefield, but her face was hard, her determination unshaken.

Stay close to me! Lewa shouted over the noise.

I can handle myself! Ife shot back, sending a wave of energy that knocked a line of guards to the ground.

Ajaka stood at the center of the chaos, his eyes locked on Ife. With a roar, he raised his hand, summoning a massive wave of golden energy that tore through the room, scattering soldiers on both sides.

Ife braced herself, countering the blast with her own energy. The collision sent shockwaves rippling through the hall, cracking the walls and shattering the ornate windows. Come on, Ife! Ajaka taunted. Show me what you're really made of! Ife gritted her teeth, her body glowing with power. She surged forward, meeting Ajaka head on. Their energies collided again, the force of it sending them both skidding backward.

You've already lost, Ajaka, Ife said, her voice cold and resolute. Step down before it's too late.

Ajaka snarled. I will never bow to you. Never!

While the battle raged on, Emperor Olorun and Empress Ayao worked their way toward Ajaka, cutting down any who stood in their way. When they finally reached him, Olorun raised his hand, signaling the soldiers to stop.

Enough! Olorun's voice rang out, commanding silence.

The fighting ceased for a moment, the soldiers on both sides halting to watch the confrontation. Ajaka turned to face his father, his chest heaving with exertion.

You've let this go on long enough, Olorun said, his tone heavy with disappointment. This isn't strength, Ajaka. This is destruction. It's time to end this madness.

Ajaka laughed bitterly. End it? For what? So, you can play Emperor again? You don't care about me, Father. You never have!

That's not true, Olorun said, his voice softening. I've always cared for you. But you've let hatred consume you, Ajaka. It's blinded you to what truly matters. What truly matters? Ajaka spat. You're a fool if you think I'll step down because you asked nicely. He turned his gaze to Ife. And you, Ife you're just like the rest of them. Thinking you're better than me. Ife stepped forward, her expression unreadable. This isn't about me, Ajaka. This is about Venus. About the people you've hurt. The people you've betrayed.

Ajaka's lips curled into a snarl. If I'm going down, I'm taking you with me.

Before anyone could react, Ajaka lunged at Ife, his energy crackling like lightning around him.

Ife met him head on, their powers colliding in a blinding explosion of light. The force of it sent everyone in the room stumbling backward, shielding their eyes.

Ajaka attacked relentlessly, his strikes fueled by rage and desperation. But Ife's movements were calculated, her training with Baka and her mother evident in every counter and every strike.

You can't win this, Ajaka! Ife shouted, her voice echoing through the hall.

I'd rather die than surrender! Ajaka roared, his attacks becoming more erratic.

As their battle raged on, Ife saw an opening. Summoning all her energy, she unleashed a powerful blast that sent Ajaka crashing into the far wall. He slumped to the ground, his breathing labored, his energy depleted.

Ife approached him cautiously, her hands still glowing with power. It's over, Ajaka. Don't make me do this. Ajaka looked up at her, his eyes filled with defiance but also a glimmer of fear. Finish it, he whispered. End it. Ife hesitated, her heart pounding. As the dust settled in the grand hall, Empress Oduwa entered her castle, her steps steady and resolute despite the chaos that had unfolded. Her gaze swept over the room, pausing on her son slumped against the wall, his body weak and his spirit shattered. She approached Ife, her eyes filled with a mix of gratitude and sorrow.

She leaned in close and whispered, Thank you, Ife. Thank you for sparing my son.

Ife's expression softened. She nodded, her voice calm but tired. No need to thank me, Your Majesty. He may have made mistakes, but I couldn't take his life. That would make me no better than him.

Empress Oduwa gave her a faint smile, then turned to face Ajaka. Her expression hardened, her regal composure returning as she addressed him firmly. Enough is enough, Ajaka.

Ajaka raised his head, glaring at his mother with a mix of defiance and confusion. Enough? he repeated bitterly. What now, Mother? You're siding with them? You're a traitor!

Empress Oduwa stepped closer, her voice unwavering. A traitor? she echoed. No, Ajaka. I am a mother, your mother. And I will not watch my only son destroy himself or our world any longer. This ends today.

Ajaka struggled to his feet, leaning against the wall for support. Or what, Mother? he spat, his voice dripping with venom. You'll punish me? For what? For wanting what's mine? For carrying on this family's legacy of hate? That's what you wanted, wasn't it? To continue the feud between our family and Empress Ayao's? I did it all for you, for our name!

Empress Oduwa's face softened for a moment, but her tone remained resolute. You did it for yourself, Ajaka. You let hate and jealousy consume you. And in doing so, you've forgotten what's truly important. She paused, her voice heavy with regret. I sent my daughter away because I listened to you. Because I let you poison my judgment. I was so blinded by anger and pride that I robbed Lewa of the love of her life. And now I've nearly lost you too, my son. But this stops now.

Ajaka's breath hitched at the mention of Lewa. His shoulders sagged, the weight of his actions finally crashing down on him. I... I only wanted to protect us, he muttered, his voice breaking. I was so consumed with hate, I forgot what mattered. I forgot what it meant to have family. I'm sorry.

Empress Oduwa stepped closer, her hands glowing softly with an ethereal light. Close your eyes, my son, she said gently but firmly.

Ajaka flinched, his instincts screaming at him to resist, but something in her tone made him obey. Slowly, he closed his eyes, his body trembling with fear and uncertainty.

Empress Oduwa's fingers lit up, the glow intensifying as she placed her hand on Ajaka's crown. A ripple of energy passed between them, and in an instant, the crown dissolved, its power dissipating into the air. Ajaka's eyes snapped open, filled with shock and betrayal.

What have you done? he whispered, his voice shaking. Empress Oduwa straightened, her regal presence commanding the room. I have taken your crown, Ajaka, she said, her tone unwavering. You no longer hold any power. You will not sit on the throne, nor will you rule over this world. That is your punishment, not death, not imprisonment, but the loss of what you value most. Ajaka stumbled backward, clutching at his head as if trying to feel the crown that was no longer there. Mother... how could you? Oduwa's voice softened, but her gaze remained steady. Because I love you, Ajaka. And I will not see my son dead or locked away in a cage. This was the only way to save you and to save Venus.

Ajaka sank to his knees, his hands trembling. I've failed you... I've failed everyone.

Empress Oduwa knelt beside him, placing a hand on his shoulder. You have a chance to start again, Ajaka. To make amends. But you must earn the trust of those you've hurt. That will be your true test.

The room fell silent as the tension dissipated, the soldiers on both sides lowering their weapons. Emperor Olorun stepped forward, his voice calm but commanding. This war is over. Let it be known that Venus will no longer be ruled by hate and division. We will rebuild not as enemies, but as one.

Ayao approached Ife, her face glowing with pride. You've done it, my daughter. You've fulfilled your purpose as the bridge between our worlds.

Ife gave her mother a faint smile, exhaustion clear in her eyes. It's not over yet, Mother. There's still so much to repair. Empress Ayao nodded. Yes. But now we can rebuild together.
Lewa stepped beside Ife, taking her hand. And I'll be by your side for every step of the way.

Ife looked at Lewa, her heart swelling with love. We'll do this together.

As the soldiers began to retreat and the castle settled into a calm quiet, Ajaka remained on his knees, his mind racing with thoughts of redemption. For the first time in centuries, the weight of his crown was gone, leaving him with the burden of reflection.

Chapter Ten: The Celebration of Venus Restored

Months turned into years, and years into centuries, as the families and citizens of Venus came together to restore their beloved planet to its former glory. The golden cities sparkled under the radiance of Venus's twin suns, and harmony returned to the lands. The feud between the Taureans and Librans became a distant memory, a lesson passed down to ensure peace for generations.

On the day of the grand celebration marking the unity of Venus, Ife and Lewa were crowned Empress Ife and Empress Lewa. Their love had become a beacon of hope, their partnership a symbol of what could be achieved when love triumphed over hate. The citizens cheered for their new Empresses, their joy echoing across the golden plains and crystalline mountains of Venus.

As the festivities carried on late into the night, Ife slipped away from the crowd to catch her breath. She wandered onto the balcony overlooking the shimmering gardens below, the cool breeze calming her racing thoughts.

Ajaka soon joined her, his steps hesitant but his expression warm. Ife, he said softly, may I speak with you?

Ife turned to him, her gaze kind. Of course, Ajaka.

He stood beside her, looking out over the celebration. I wanted to apologize to you again. For everything.

Ife gave a small laugh. Ajaka, you've been apologizing for a century now. I forgave you a long time ago. He smiled, the guilt in his eyes softening. Thank you. You've always been more gracious than I deserved. Ife hesitated, you know, you're more than worthy of having your crown back. You've earned it a hundred times over.

Ajaka shook his head. I'm not the one who should wear it, Ife.

Ajaka chuckled, rubbing the back of his neck. I'm better off without it, to be honest. That's why I told Mother to give it to Lewa. If it wasn't for her finding you all those centuries ago, none of this would've been possible.

Ife smiled, gratitude warming her chest. She is incredible, isn't she?

Before Ajaka could respond, Lewa stepped onto the balcony, her presence grounding Ife instantly. She rested a hand on Ife's arm and smiled at her brother.

I was wondering where you'd wandered off to, Lewa teased gently. Then her tone softened as she turned to Ife. Are you alright, my love?

Ife hesitated, her gaze drifting to the stars. Lewa... Ajaka, how long has it been since I left Earth?

Ajaka frowned, calculating in his head. It's been a century here on Venus," he said slowly. Back on Earth, that would be about... 22,500 days.

Ife's breath caught. So, what you're saying is... my family, my friends, Ishara, they're gone? Her voice broke. They've all passed.

Lewa tightened her grip on Ife's arm, her voice calm and soothing. My love, they lived full lives. And they loved you deeply. But I need to tell you something. Ife's head snapped toward Lewa, her eyes wide. What is it? Lewa hesitated for only a moment. Before we returned to Venus, I sent Lemanja to Earth. I asked her to wipe their memories of you.

What? Ife whispered, her voice trembling. Why would you do that?

Lewa's expression was gentle, her voice steady. Because they missed you too much. Ishara prayed for your return every night. Your mother, your siblings they grieved for you constantly. I didn't want them to suffer, knowing you would never return.

Ife's heart ached, but she nodded, understanding Lewa's reasoning. You did that... for me?

Lewa reached into her robes and pulled out a small, weathered photograph. I also kept this for you. It's a picture of you all from that day in the park, before I found you. I knew you would remember them one day, and I thought you'd want to have it.

Ife took the photograph with trembling hands. The image showed her with her earthly family her mother, her siblings, Bryce, and Ishara, all laughing and carefree. Tears welled in her eyes as she clutched it to her chest.

Looking to the sky, she whispered, wherever you all are, I love you. I miss you. Thank you for everything.

Lewa placed a hand on her back, her touch warm and steady. I only wanted to keep you happy, my love, she said softly. Ife turned to her, smiling through her tears. Thank you, Lewa. For understanding what they meant to me. Lewa leaned in, pressing a gentle kiss to Ife's lips. Ajaka, who had been silently watching, cleared his throat with a sheepish smile. I was a fool to think I could keep you two apart, he admitted. What was I thinking all those centuries ago?

Ife laughed, wiping her tears. I'm glad you've come around, Ajaka.

Ajaka chuckled and bowed his head. Enjoy the rest of the celebration, my empresses. He turned and walked back inside, leaving them alone on the balcony.

Later that night, after the festivities had ended, Ife and Lewa found themselves in the golden garden. The stars shone brightly above them, their light reflecting off the shimmering petals of the trees. They sat together on the soft grass, their hands intertwined.

Lewa turned to Ife, her voice soft and curious. Can I ask you something, my love?

Of course, Ife replied, her head resting on Lewa's shoulder.

What made you choose me? Lewa asked. You could've gone back to Earth. To Ishara. To your family there. Why did you stay?

Ife lifted her head and gazed at Lewa, her eyes filled with love. The night you came to my room on Mercury, she began, her voice steady, when you apologized and told me you'd rather lose me, than have me upset with you, that's when I knew. Anyone who's willing to let go of the love of their life, just to see them happy... that person must be the one.

Ife paused, brushing a hand against Lewa's cheek. I loved Ishara, but she wasn't my life mate. I belong here with you. Lewa smiled, tears glistening in her eyes. And I'm with you, my love. Always. Under the light of Venus's twin moons, they leaned into each other, their lips meeting in a passionate kiss. The stars above seemed to shine brighter, as if blissing their union.

And in that moment, surrounded by the beauty of their restored home, Ife and Lewa found peace, knowing that together, they were stronger than anything the universe could throw at them.

Lewa leaned close to Ife, her breath warm against her ear. I have one more surprise for you, my love.

Ife smiled, her curiosity piqued. Another surprise? What is it?

Lewa stood and extended her hand. Follow me.

Intrigued, Ife let Lewa lead her through the golden garden and toward the spacecraft docked nearby. Where are we going? Ife asked, a playful smile tugging at her lips

Lewa shot her a mysterious look. You'll see.

Once aboard the craft, Lewa turned to the captain. Stay the course and head to Jupiter.

Ife raised an eyebrow in surprise. Jupiter? Are we going shopping? She laughed lightly, shaking her head. I haven't been to Jupiter in millennia.

The journey to Jupiter was swift, the ship soaring through the stars until they reached the planet's vibrant atmosphere. The colors of the swirling gas storms and shimmering moons filled Ife's vision, a sight she had almost forgotten. The craft landed in a secure area on the planet's surface, near a quiet town surrounded by crystalline structures and lush fields.

As they disembarked and walked into the town, Ife looked around, her confusion growing. Lewa, what are we doing here?

Before Lewa could answer, a Jupiterian man stepped out of his home with his wife and children. The man's energy hit Ife like a wave warm, familiar, and unmistakable. She froze, her heart pounding in her chest. Slowly, she turned to Lewa, her voice trembling. No... you didn't.

Lewa's lips curved into a gentle smile. Oh, yes, I did.

Ife's eyes filled with tears as she whispered, Is that...?

Lewa nodded. Yup. That's your dad.

Ife's tears spilled over as she watched the man approach them, a friendly smile on his face. He noticed her crying and immediately stepped closer. His voice was calm and kind. Are you ladies, okay?

Ife wiped at her tears, her smile trembling. Yeah, she managed. These are tears of joy.

The man tilted his head, studying her for a moment. Alright. I was just checking. I'd hate to see a lady upset. Ife smiled through her tears. I know you wouldn't, she said softly, but her words carried a deeper meaning she didn't dare explain. The man's brows furrowed slightly as he looked closer at her. Do I know you? He asked. I feel like I know you. Ife's heart ached, but she smiled warmly. Maybe in another life.

The man returned the smile, nodding as if that made perfect sense. Yeah. I believe that. He paused, glancing down thoughtfully before asking, are you close to your dad?

Ife's voice trembled. I was. But he was taken away too soon.

The man's expression softened, and he hesitated for a moment before stepping forward. I don't know why, but... I feel like I'm supposed to give you a hug. Would that be, okay?

Ife nodded, her voice barely above a whisper. Sure.

As the man embraced her, Ife closed her eyes, feeling the warmth of his energy the same energy she had longed for all these years.

As he pulled back, he smiled at her, his voice gentle. Wherever your dad is, he'd be so proud of you. And he loves you dearly.

Ife's tears fell freely now, and she whispered, Thank you.

The man's wife called out to him from their car. Honey, is everything alright?

He turned and smiled reassuringly. Yeah. I just felt led to speak with this young lady for some reason. The woman smiled, nodding. Oh, okay, honey. Ife took a deep breath, her voice steadying as she said, Thank you. For everything. Enjoy your family. The man nodded, his kind smile never fading. Same to you. Have a nice day.

As he climbed into his car and drove away with his family, Ife watched until they disappeared. She turned her gaze to the sky and whispered, I love you, Dad.

Lewa stepped closer, wrapping an arm around Ife's waist. You are amazing, my love, Lewa said softly.

Ife turned to her, her tears now mixed with a smile. No, you are. She cupped Lewa's face and kissed her deeply, pouring every ounce of gratitude and love into the moment. I love you, Lewa.

And I love you, Lewa replied, her voice tender. She grinned mischievously. Now! let's go shopping.

THE END...

www.ingramcontent.com/pod-product-compliance
Lightning Source LLC
Chambersburg PA
CBHW080750250626
47162CB00011B/3087